FGHIJK

QRSTU

ABCDE

LMNOP

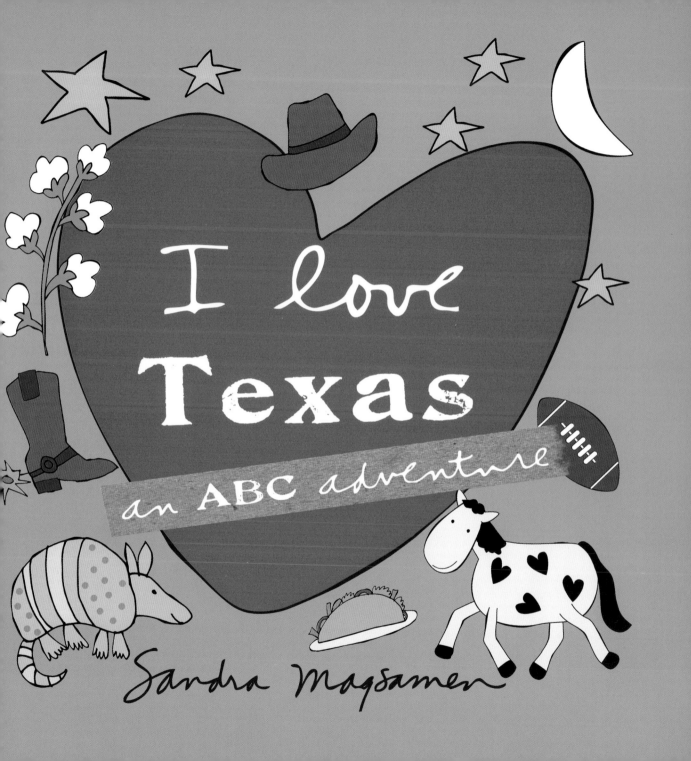

I love Texas

an ABC adventure

Sandra Magsamen

Texas is filled with fantastic and beautiful things to see and do. Just follow the **A, B, C's,** there is an amazing adventure waiting for you!

The Lone Star State

Amarillo

texas the friendship state

Dallas

El Paso

Austin
(state capital)

Houston

San Antonio

Galveston

A is for armadillo.

Watch it as it waddles and makes its way.

B is for the **bluebonnet.** Our state flower will brighten every day.

C is for cowboys

who ride horses and herd cattle across the land.

D is for dude ranches

where awesome outdoor adventures are at hand.

E is for El Paso's great river raft race on the Rio Grande each year.

F is for football.

The Dallas Cowboys are a team to root for and cheer!

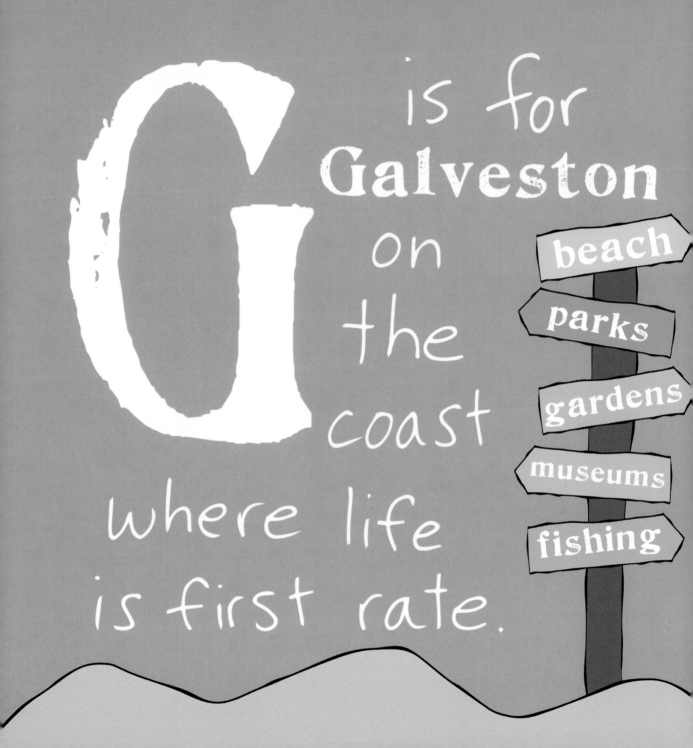

G is for
Galveston
on
the
coast
where life
is first rate.

beach

parks

gardens

museums

fishing

H is for the **Houston Astros.** Our baseball team is great!

I is for what the **incredible** State Aquarium can teach.

J is for **jumping** through all the fun blue waves on a Gulf Shore beach.

K

is for **kayaking**

down the Brazos River that's long and flowing

L is for the **Lone Star State,** where fields of cotton are always growing.

O is for the **orca whales** at SeaWorld who swim all day.

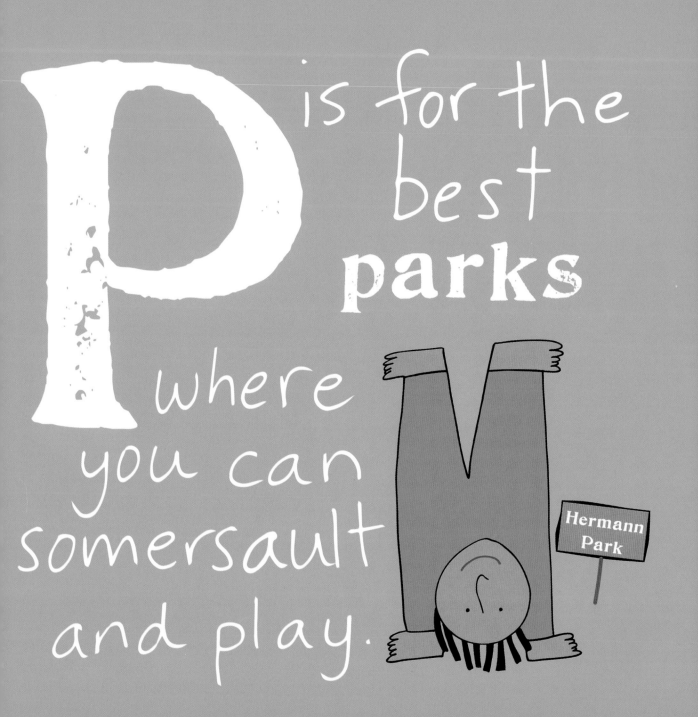

Q

is for **quietly** gazing at the stars that shine bright.

R is for rodeo,

where paint horses run fast as light.

S is for Sunshine.

Our state is so warm and nice.

T is for tacos.

They're great with black beans and rice.

U is for united

Texas the friendship state

because in Texas the best friendships are made.

V is for the violins at the Austin Philharmonic being played.

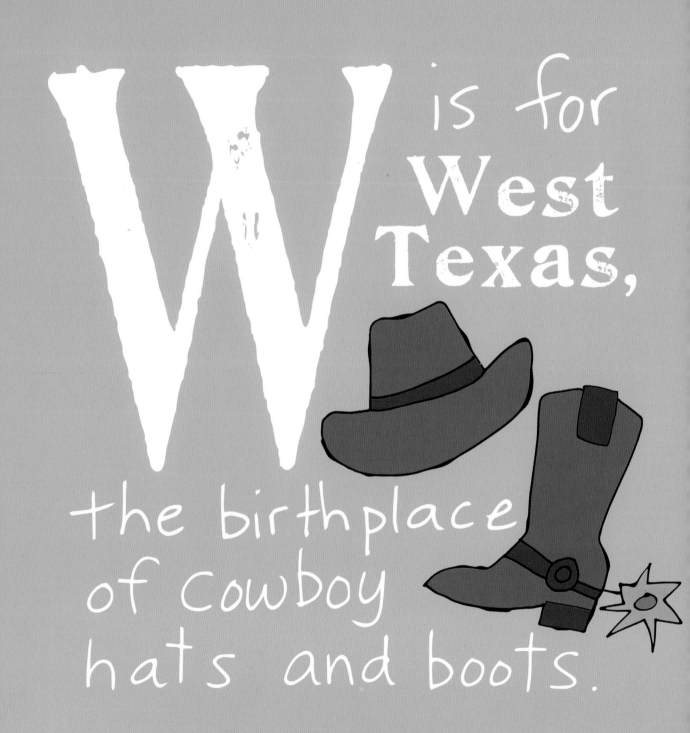

W is for West Texas,

the birthplace of cowboy hats and boots.

X is for XOXO

because we love having Texan roots!

Z is for the **ZOO** where grey sea lions swim along.

Austin Zoo

adventure

an end,
can go
A and
again!

Sandra Magsamen is a best-selling and award-winning artist, author, and designer whose meaningful and message-driven art has touched millions of lives, one heart at a time. She loves to travel and has had many awesome adventures around the world. For now, she lives happily and artfully in Vermont with her family and their dog, Olive.

A big thank you to my amazing studio team of Hannah Barry and Karen Botti. Their creativity, research tenacity and spirit of adventure have been invaluable as we crafted the ABC adventure series.

Sandra Magsamen

Text and illustrations © 2015 Hanny Girl Productions, Inc. www.sandramagsamen.com
Exclusively represented by Mixed Media Group, Inc. NY, NY.
Cover and internal design © 2015 by Sandra Magsamen

Sourcebooks and the colophon are registered trademarks of Sourcebooks, Inc.

Published by Sourcebooks Jabberwocky, an imprint of Sourcebooks, Inc.
P.O. Box 4410, Naperville, Illinois 60567-4410
(630) 961-3900
Fax: (630) 961-2168
www.sourcebooks.com

Library of Congress Cataloging-in-Publication data is on file with the publisher.

Source of Production: Leo Paper, Heshan City, Guangdong Province, China
Date of Production: July 2015
Run Number: 5004061

Printed and bound in China.
LEO 10 9 8 7 6 5 4 3 2 1

ABCDE
LMNOP
VWXYZ
FGHIJK